Someday Cyril

Someday Cyril

by **Phillis Gershator**

illustrated by
Cedric Lucas

MONDO

For information contact:
Mondo Publishing
980 Avenue of Americas
New York, NY 10018

MONDO is a registered trademark of Mondo Publishing
Visit our web site at http://www.mondopub.com
Printed in the United States of America
02 03 04 05 06   9 8 7 6 5 4 3 2

Design by Mina Greenstein
Production by The Kids at Our House

ISBN 1-57255-748-6

To Daniel, David, Aldo, Jean,
my editor Louise May, and all the KATS kids
and volunteer instructors
—P.G.

To my family, friends, and
to all who inspire
—C.L.

Contents

Too Busy

Cyril lived on the island of St. Thomas. Even though he was surrounded by water, Cyril had never once been out to sea—not on a raft, a ferry, or a sailboat. And he wanted to go on a boat more than anything.

When Cyril asked his parents about going on a boat, all they would say was, "Maybe someday."

Cyril didn't like the words *maybe* and *someday*. *Maybe* and *someday* did not mean *yes* and *today*.

"What if *maybe* and *someday* really mean *no* and *never*," Cyril grumbled. He kicked the leg of a dining room chair.

The chair wobbled and fell on its side with a thump.

Today is a perfectly good day to go out on a boat, Cyril thought. *But no, everybody is too busy.*

Mama was busy feeding his baby sister, Lora. Papa was busy repairing the dining room chairs. All the chairs were wobbly.

Cyril sat down hard on another chair.

"Cyril, can't you see I'm busy?" Papa said. "Why don't you . . ."

Before Papa could finish what he was saying, Uncle Elvin drove up in his big blue taxi van. "Good morning," Uncle Elvin called. "What's happening?"

His uncle was so cheerful, Cyril couldn't stay grumpy. "Hi, Uncle Elvin," Cyril said. "Everybody is busy. But not me. Can I sit in your van?"

"Sure," said Uncle Elvin. "Come on up."

Cyril hopped into the van, next to Uncle Elvin. Sitting in the front seat, up high, Cyril felt very important and grown-up.

"Everybody is busy?" Uncle Elvin repeated. "Well, maybe I can help out. Let's go see."

Papa said yes, he could use Uncle Elvin's help fixing the chairs. And he could use Cyril's help, too.

"Cyril," Papa said, "please bring Uncle Elvin and me some ice water."

Cyril brought out a jug of ice water and some glasses. Then he walked in a circle around Uncle Elvin's van, admiring it. He imagined being a taxi driver. He would make lots of money driving visitors around St.

11

Thomas in his big van. He would show them the old fort and the shops and the best beaches on the island, just like Uncle Elvin did.

All the imaginary driving, especially driving to the beach, made Cyril thirsty. He went to pour himself a glass of ice water. That's when he overheard Papa and Uncle Elvin talking. They were talking about going fishing in Uncle Elvin's new boat, a little 14-foot Boston Whaler.

Then they started talking about *him*.

"Do you think Cyril could handle a whole day at sea?" Uncle Elvin asked Papa.

"Maybe," Papa said. "He's eight already. I think he could."

Was Cyril ever glad he was eight.

"Would you like to go out with us on the boat tomorrow, Cyril?" Papa asked.

Would he? "Yes!" Cyril shouted.

"It might be a long day," Papa warned.

"It won't be long for me," Cyril promised.

Mama was worried though. "Is it safe?

Do you have life jackets?" she asked. "How long will you be gone?"

"Of course it's safe," Uncle Elvin said. "And of course we'll take life jackets. We should be back at the Red Hook Marina by six o'clock. If we're not, my friend Hank will send the Coast Guard out to look for us. But don't worry. Everything is going to be fine."

"Don't forget, Mama, I can dog paddle," Cyril reminded her.

Cyril had learned to swim at Coki Beach. He wasn't about to drown at sea. Besides, if the boat tipped over, he would be wearing one of Uncle Elvin's orange life jackets. And if the coast guard didn't rescue them, they could swim to the shore of a deserted island and live on crabs, sea grapes, and rain water.

Cyril secretly hoped the boat would tip over. Then they would be shipwrecked. Just like in the movies!

Boat Trip

"Climb aboard," Uncle Elvin said. Cyril sat at one end of the boat. Uncle Elvin sat at the other end. Papa sat in the middle.

Uncle Elvin started up the motor. They were off! Before long, St. Thomas looked like a little green hill bobbing in the blue, blue sea. There were more islands ahead, one island after another. The boat passed close to a steep one. Waves hit the cliffs so hard, white spray rose up like smoke against the rocks. The boat tipped from side to side in the choppy water.

"Do you have any matches, Uncle Elvin?" Cyril asked.

"What do we need matches for?" Uncle Elvin replied.

"If we're shipwrecked, we might need them to start a fire so we can cook the crabs," said Cyril.

"We won't be shipwrecked. The water is not *that* choppy," Uncle Elvin said.

Uncle Elvin stopped the motor. They fished for an hour, but the fish weren't biting. So Uncle Elvin started up the motor

again and headed out to a small island with a sandy white beach. Papa and Uncle Elvin pulled the boat halfway up onto the sand.

Cyril was glad they wouldn't be shipwrecked on *this* island. He didn't see any sea grape trees. Not even a coconut palm. Nothing to eat. Just short, scrubby bush with tough leaves only a goat could chew.

They were the only people on the island. But someone had been there before them.

"Look, a broken-down wood shack!" Cyril cried. "And look, somebody made a campfire. Papa, Uncle Elvin, somebody was shipwrecked here! It must have been a pirate. With treasure! I bet the pirate buried treasure on this island."

Cyril wanted to dig for the treasure, but he hadn't brought along a shovel. How was he to know they would end up on a pirate's beach?

Papa and Uncle Elvin stretched out for a rest. Cyril didn't feel like resting.

"We didn't catch any fish yet," Cyril said. "There's a pelican diving over there. I bet the pelican caught a fish."

Uncle Elvin sat up, shading his eyes with his hand as he looked at the sparkling sea. "Cyril, you have sharp eyes," he said. "Pelicans and fish go together."

Sure enough, whole schools of tiny sprat and fry were swimming close to shore.

"Look at that! Let's throw out a net and catch some sprat," Uncle Elvin said.

After they had pulled in a load of silvery fish, it was time to go. They chugged along, keeping clear of the coral reef, until—*chucka, chucka, chucka*—the motor sputtered. And then—*chuck, chuck*—the motor choked up and died.

Out of Gas

They were out of gas!

The spare gas container was empty, too. And there was only one oar in the boat.

"Will we be shipwrecked?" Cyril asked.

"I hope not," Uncle Elvin said.

Cyril also hoped they wouldn't be shipwrecked, not without a shovel.

"What do we do now?" he asked.

"Wind power," said Uncle Elvin.

Uncle Elvin tied the oar to the side of the boat. The oar became the mast. Then he tied his shirt to the top. The shirt became the sail. But the sail was too small. The "sailboat" just drifted slowly along.

"All right, it's time to paddle!" ordered Uncle Elvin. They paddled as fast as they could with their hands and one oar.

The boat inched along across the place where the waters of the Atlantic Ocean and the Caribbean Sea meet. The currents made the waves swell and the boat rock. They all breathed a sigh of relief when they got past the rough currents.

"We made it!" cried Cyril as they pulled into the Cruz Bay dock in St. John.

Uncle Elvin tied up the boat and they headed for the gas station. Uncle Elvin carried his red plastic gas container.

"I should have filled this before we left," he admitted.

"Well, we'll fill it now," Cyril said, taking big steps to keep up with the grownups.

By the time they got back to the marina in St. Thomas, the sun was going down. Uncle Elvin's friend Hank was upset. "It's late!" he yelled. "Where were you? We were about to call the Coast Guard."

And then, when they got home, Mama scolded them. "You're late!" she said. "I was worried about you."

Cyril didn't know why Hank and Mama were making such a fuss.

"We had fun," Cyril said. "We caught a bunch of sprat and fry. And you know what? It was a good thing I went along because I'm the one who saw the pelican."

That night Cyril made a wish on the first star. He wished for another boat trip. Planning ahead, he made a list. They would need two oars next time, a full container of gas, and a shovel for digging up the buried treasure.

Pirates Day

For the next few weeks, Uncle Elvin had a lot of taxi driving to do. He didn't have any time to go out on his boat.

"Someday," he promised Cyril.

"*Someday* again," grumbled Cyril. "That could mean another eight years from now."

But even if Cyril couldn't go out on a boat, he could watch the boats in the harbor on Pirates Day.

The people on St. Thomas didn't celebrate Pirates Day every year. But this year two big sailing ships were going to have a make-believe battle in the harbor. The crew on each boat would dress up like pirates. Then they would try to board the "enemy" ship and take captives. After the battle, the other sailboats would set sail, too, with their black pirate flags flying in the breeze.

Cyril's neighbor, Miss Elsie, had a nephew who owned a sailboat. "I'll ask Armand about Pirates Day," she promised.

Maybe, Cyril hoped, he would be really lucky. Maybe he wouldn't have to wait eight years for another boat trip.

Armand agreed to take Cyril and his family out on his boat for the Pirates Day sail. Miss Elsie didn't want to go. She said sailing made her queasy. She offered to stay home and take care of Lora instead.

Cyril was lucky. First a Boston Whaler, and now a sailboat. A real sailboat with real sails, not a shirt tied to an oar.

It didn't matter if you ran out of gas on a real sailboat. The wind could carry you along. You could go from island to island, across the high seas, all across the Atlantic Ocean if you wanted to. And you could do it without a drop of gas. Cyril only hoped he wouldn't get queasy like Miss Elsie.

On Pirates Day, Cyril wolfed down his breakfast. He was the first one dressed and ready to go. He wore short, raggedy jeans and a striped T-shirt. A cardboard cutlass hung at his side. He borrowed a gold-colored earring from his mother to clip on one ear,

because pirates always wore one gold earring.

Cyril's family met Armand on the waterfront. "Ahoy there," Armand called. "Welcome aboard the *Sea Bird*."

From Armand's little sailboat anchored in the harbor, they watched the battle between the two big sailboats. One boat had red sails. The other boat had white sails. Everyone was shouting and yelling. Smoke bombs filled the air with white smoke. Flare guns blasted like firecrackers. Just like in the movies. Even better!

A loud cheer went up. The boat with white sails had won the battle. The flag on the boat with red sails was lowered. A flag with a skull and crossbones rose in its place. Then all the other sailboats hoisted their pirate flags and headed out to sea.

Armand started up the motor on his sailboat. Once they got out of the crowded harbor, he turned off the motor. Then the sails did the work, as long as Armand ran back and forth adjusting them.

"This is the way to go," said Mama. "It's peaceful and quiet. No noise from a motor."

"We're part of nature," Cyril said. "We're part of the sky and the water."

Cyril felt great, not queasy at all. He felt like a flying fish. He felt like a bird skimming across the sea.

Like a bird, Armand's boat was small but fast. "I race to St. John in this boat," he told Cyril. "And I usually win."

"If the wind blows all the boats the same way, wouldn't the race be a tie?" Cyril asked.

"No," Armand replied. "It depends on

how you use the wind. That's why I move the sails in different directions, to keep up speed and keep on course."

Cyril wanted to learn to move the sails around, but for now he just tried to stay out of Armand's way.

They sailed by an island with a nice

beach. "This is a good place to swim," Armand said. "I'll anchor out here. You can take the lifeboat into shore and go for a swim."

Cyril stayed to keep Armand company on the *Sea Bird*. He watched the others paddle out to the beach and jump into the water. It looked like fun. He began to wish he had gone, too. But by then it was too late. Armand was already waving to the swimmers to come back.

They quickly paddled back to the sailboat. "Here, hold the paddles," Papa said, handing them up to Cyril from the lifeboat. "Good. Now hold onto the rope."

Cyril held tight to the rope while everyone climbed aboard the *Sea Bird*. Papa climbed up the ladder last. He took the rope from Cyril.

"I'll tie it up," Papa said. But all of a sudden he sneezed, and the rope slipped from his hands.

"Oh, no!" Papa cried.

They stared at the lifeboat floating away. If they lost the lifeboat, Cyril was afraid Armand would be sorry he took them sailing. If they lost the lifeboat, Armand would never invite them on his boat again.

"I'll get it!" Cyril shouted, jumping overboard.

Cyril paddled as fast as he could toward the rubber boat. He almost had it. No, not yet. The lifeboat kept bobbing away, just out of reach.

"Slow down, lifeboat!" Cyril yelled. He kicked harder and tried again. "Gotcha!" he cried, and hung on tight.

Armand sailed the *Sea Bird* closer to Cyril. Cyril clung to the lifeboat until it was safely tied up. Then he paddled over to the ladder. Armand helped him onto the deck.

"Thanks. Thanks a lot!" said Armand. "That was quick thinking, Sailor Cyril."

Cyril's sneakers were waterlogged and his cutlass was soggy, but he had saved the day. He felt like a hero. Best of all, Armand had called him sailor. Armand might even invite him to go sailing again.

More than anything, Cyril wanted to go out on a sailboat again. And he wanted, someday, to sail it himself.

KATS

"Good morning, Cyril," said Papa, pulling the sheet off Cyril's bed.

"Good morning," Cyril mumbled.

It was still early. Cyril could see the pinkish clouds outside his window. That meant the sun was just coming up.

Was today a school day? No, today was Saturday and Saturday wasn't a school day. Why was Papa waking him up so early?

"Cyril, do you know about KATS?" Papa asked.

"Sure. Cats *meow*. They like to eat fish. Why, Papa?" Cyril sat up. "Are we getting a cat?"

"No. I'm talking about K-A-T-S—Kids and the Sea," Papa explained. "Armand called last night and told us about Kids and the Sea. He said you might like to join up. He thought you would make a good sailor."

"He did?" Cyril jumped out of bed, wide awake. "What do I have to do?"

"Go to classes on Saturday mornings," said Papa. "So, if you want to be a KATS kid, let's get moving."

Cyril and Papa caught an early ferry to St. John. Cyril's heart beat faster as the boat pulled away from the dock.

Once they were on the open sea, the wind kicked up. The ferry lurched up and down over the choppy water.

"Look at those waves!" Papa exclaimed.

"I feel them," Cyril said. "It sure is windy."

How will I ever learn to sail on such a windy day? Cyril thought. He imagined the ropes whipping out of his hands, the sails swinging back and forth, the boat flipping over. Armand said he would be a good sailor, but how could he prove it if he capsized the first time out?

Cyril and Papa took the bus from the ferry dock along the winding, hilly roads down to Coral Bay. When they got there, Cyril walked around, waiting for his class to begin. He saw boats piled up on wood racks.

"Are those the boats for beginners?" he asked one of the older boys.

"No way. Those are Lasers. If you're a beginner, you start with prams and Sunfish," the boy said.

"I'm a beginner," said Cyril. "Where are the prams and Sunfish?"

"If you're a beginner-beginner, you don't go sailing on anything yet," explained the boy. "You have to learn all kinds of stuff first."

"What?" Cyril's mouth dropped open. "No sailing today?"

The boy shook his head. "It takes weeks before you go out."

Cyril looked so disappointed, the boy said, "You'll get to go out in a rowboat pretty soon."

Cyril cheered up. He knew how to row.

He had already rowed in a Boston Whaler.
The instructor would see what a good rower
he was and let him go sailing in no time.

That wasn't the way it worked.

Pete, one of the instructors, told Cyril
and the other beginners they had to learn
the safety rules first. "We'll start with the

two most important ones," Pete said. "Always wear your life jacket and always stay with your boat, even if it turns over."

"You'll also be learning to tie knots, rig the boat, work the sails, and speak a new language—boat language," said Jan, another instructor. "So let's get started."

Jan held up flash cards for the new words. Some were old words with new meanings. The cards were tricky. One had the word STERN printed on it with a picture of a frowning face.

"The back of the boat," Cyril shouted.

The next tricky card had the word BOW with a picture of a bow and arrow.

"The front of the boat," shouted Tim, the boy sitting next to Cyril.

They practiced using a silent boat language, too, in case the wind, waves, and flapping sails made too much noise for people to hear each other. Arms up meant "I need help." Two fingers forming a circle meant "I'm okay."

On the way back to the ferry, Papa said,

"It's a long trip to get here. Are you sure you want to do this every week?"

"Oh yes, Papa!" said Cyril. "But you don't have to come. Tim lives on St. John. His mother takes him. He said they could pick me up at the ferry dock."

"Well, if you're sure . . ." Papa said.

"I'm sure, Papa," said Cyril. "I want to sail more than anything. Then I can race a boat. They have races for kids. Maybe I'll win a sailboat race!"

From then on, every Saturday morning Cyril took the ferry by himself. He met his KATS buddy Tim at the dock. After class, he took the ferry back to St. Thomas. Sometimes Papa picked him up. And sometimes Uncle Elvin came in his big blue taxi van. That was fine with Cyril. He got to sit high up in the front seat right next to his uncle.

At last, the great day arrived, the day Cyril had been waiting for.

Captain Cyril

"**E**verybody sails today," said Pete.

Cyril's group piled into a truck. Pete drove them to Johnson's Bay, where KATS kept the beginner boats. Some of the instructors were already spreading small rugs in the sand to protect the bottoms of the boats.

Everyone pitched in to lift the boats off the racks. First they lifted the Sunfish, with their brightly colored sails, and then the prams, with their white sails and squared-off bows.

Cyril and Tim helped put up the mast on their boat. They tied down the red and yellow sail. Then they attached the rudder to the stern and the tiller to the rudder.

"Okay, kids, give it the old heave ho," Pete said.

Tim and Cyril helped Pete and Jan carry the Sunfish into the water. The boys sat on one side of the boat and Pete sat on the other. Pete slipped the centerboard into a slot in the front end.

"Tie it down," Pete said. "Do you remember why?"

40

Cyril remembered. "We don't want the centerboard to get lost if the boat flips over. We need it to help right the boat," he said.

"Can we, Pete?" Tim begged. "Can we capsize? Just for practice. Please."

"Not this time," said Pete. "Let's do some sailing first. Who wants to steer?"

"Me!" Tim said.

"Okay, Tim," Pete agreed. "You take the tiller. Cyril, you've got the sheet."

Cyril gave the "okay" using his fingers. He held tight to the sheet, the rope that held the sail. Pete told him when to let the sail out and when to pull it in. It wasn't hard. Someday he would be able to hold the sheet and steer at the same time.

"Whoops!" Pete shouted, throwing a water jug overboard. "What do we do now? Save it or leave it?"

Leave it? NO! It was time to practice the "crew overboard" drill.

First they sailed away from the jug, making a circle. On the way back, Cyril reached out to grab the jug—and missed.

They made another loop. This time Tim reached out.

"Got it!" he cried.

"Good save," said Pete. "Now, are you ready to try a real crew overboard?"

"I'll go," Cyril said quickly. He wanted to make up for not catching the water jug.

Cyril dropped into the water feet first. His life jacket made it easy to float. But even with the life jacket, being the person overboard was a little scary.

Cyril watched the boat pulling away from him. He didn't panic. He knew the boat would turn and come back alongside him as fast as possible. But how would he feel if he had really fallen overboard? More than a little scared.

Cyril pretended to cry for help. He waved his arms. "Help! Help! Don't leave me here. Come back, Tim!"

The boat headed towards him. "I'm coming! I'm coming!" Tim called. "Take it easy. Don't panic. I'll save you!"

Now Tim held the sheet and Pete steered the boat. "Ease the sail, Tim," said Pete.

The boat slowed down and Tim reached out to help Cyril climb aboard.

"Good work, boys," Pete said.

Pete slid over so Cyril could take a turn at the tiller. Cyril guided the boat back to shore. He remembered to steer left when he wanted the boat to go right.

Back in shallow surf, they untied the centerboard and pulled it up. Pete took down the mast. Cyril and Tim jumped out to help carry the boat onto the sand. After they detached the tiller and rudder, they tied the sail neatly to the mast. The boat was ready to slide back into its place on the rack.

Then Tim and Cyril grabbed a rug. They dunked it in the water to rinse off the sand.

"I hope we get to capsize next time," Tim said.

"Me, too," said Cyril. "I'm ready."

A real sailor had to be ready for

anything—a sudden wind, a broken tiller, a capsized boat. And Cyril was going to be a real sailor. Someday.

Someday wasn't such a bad word after all. It didn't mean *never*. And it could mean *soon*. Very soon.

What is KATS?

KATS stands for Kids and the Sea. It is an organization that teaches children boating and marine safety.

In 1986, three young boys who lived in the Virgin Islands drowned in a boating accident. People were very sad and upset. They wanted to prevent a tragedy like that from ever happening again. That's when KATS was born.

Hundreds of children ages 8 to 18 have taken classes and been KATS kids over the years. They have learned to sail a variety of boats safely. Some of the volunteer KATS instructors are prize-winning sailors themselves.

For more information about KATS, contact the organization at:

P.O. Box 9901
St. John, U.S. Virgin Islands 00830-9726
e-mail:katsstjohn@hotmail.com

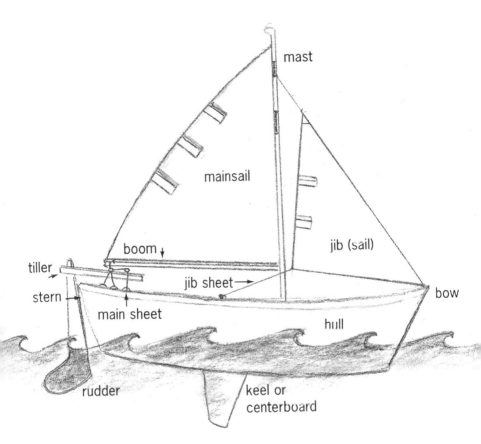

mast

mainsail

boom

tiller

stern

main sheet

jib sheet

jib (sail)

bow

hull

rudder

keel or
centerboard

SAILBOAT

PHILLIS GERSHATOR is the author of many picture books, including *Sweet, Sweet Fig Banana* and *ZZZNG! ZZZNG! ZZZNG!* and one other Cyril book, *Sugar Cakes Cyril*. *Someday Cyril* was inspired by real people and events on the beautiful island of St. Thomas in the U.S. Virgin Islands, where Ms. Gershator lives and has worked as a children's librarian. Before that, she was a children's librarian with the Brooklyn Public Library in New York.

The author says she hopes that everybody's *someday* become a *one day*.

CEDRIC LUCAS is the chairperson of a middle school art department, and his interest in art led him into illustrating children's books. Among the books he has illustrated are *Frederick Douglass: The Last Day of Slavery*, *Night Golf*, *Crab Man*, and the first Cyril book, *Sugar Cakes Cyril*. His work also appears in *America, the Beautiful*, a collection of poetry.

Mr. Lucas lives in Yonkers, New York, with his wife and two children, all of whom serve as a great inspiration for his work.